Other Awesome Animal titles available:

Meerkat Madness

More Meerkat Madness

Meerkat Madness: Flying High

Merry Meerkat Madness

Penguin Pandemonium

Penguin Pandemonium: The Rescue

Panda Panic

Panda Panic: Running Wild

Raccoon Rampage

Raccoon Rampage: The Raid

Koala Calamity

Coming Soon:

Llama Drama

Penguin Pandemonium: The Snow Beast

Koala Calamity: Surf's Up!

Otter Chaos!

KOALA CALAMITY

JONATHAN MERES

Illustrated by Neal Layton

HarperCollins *Children's Books*

First published in Great Britain by HarperCollins *Children's Books* in 2013
HarperCollins Children's Books is a division of HarperCollins*Publishers* Ltd,
77-85 Fulham Palace Road, Hammersmith, London, W6 8JB.

Visit us on the web at
www.harpercollins.co.uk

1

978-0-00-749079-0
Printed and bound in England by Clays Ltd, St Ives plc

MIX
Paper from
responsible sources
FSC® C007454

FSC™ is a non-profit international organisation established to promote
the responsible management of the world's forests. Products carrying the
FSC label are independently certified to assure consumers that they come
from forests that are managed to meet the social, economic and
ecological needs of present and future generations,
and other controlled sources.

Find out more about HarperCollins and the environment at
www.harpercollins.co.uk/green

To Molly love from Johnny

Chapter One

It was the crack of dawn at The Acacia Koala Sanctuary. Things were beginning to stir. Wings were beginning to whir. But high in the treetops, Dude and Bro were still busy doing what Dude and Bro did best. Absolutely nothing. Zilch. Nada.

Koalas are, by nature, extremely lazy. But best buddies Dude and Bro had taken this laziness to a whole new level. If sleeping had been an Olympic sport, Dude and Bro would have won hands down. Or paws down, anyway. If they could have been bothered. Which they probably couldn't. But you get the picture. The fact that it was morning meant nothing to Dude and Bro. They didn't know if it was the crack of dawn, or the crack of noon. And frankly, they didn't care either.

"Pass me another eucy branch, Dude," said Bro, stifling a yawn.

"What's that, Bro?" said Dude, stifling an even bigger one.

"I said, pass me another eucy branch. I'm done with this one."

"Are you kidding me?" said Dude. "Fetch it yourself."

"Aw, Dude, c'mon," said Bro.

"No way, Bro!" said Dude.

Bro sighed. It was by far the most energetic thing he'd done that day. "Final answer?"

"Final answer," said Dude.

Bro was not happy. He was even less happy a moment later when the sun went behind a cloud, casting him in cool shadow. And it had been such a beautiful morning until then!

"G'day!" said a voice.

Bro just about managed to crank open one eye. It was the *second* most energetic thing he'd done that day. But at least he now knew that the sun hadn't really gone behind a cloud. It was just his annoying little brother, Squirt, blocking it from view. And if Bro had anything to do with it, he wouldn't be blocking it for much longer.

"Out the way, Squirt!" snarled Bro. "I'm colder than a penguin's bum, here!"

"You could at least be a little bit grateful," said Squirt.

"Oh, yeah?" said Bro. "And why's that then?"

"Ta-da!" said Squirt, producing a particularly delicious-looking eucalyptus branch from behind his back, like a magician conjuring up a bunch of flowers.

In a shot, *both* of Bro's eyes were wide open. "Why didn't you say so in the first place, ya wallaby?"

"You're welcome," grinned Squirt, handing his big brother the branch.

"If that's all you came here to do, you can clear off again," said Bro.

"Aw, Bro," said Dude, winking at Squirt. "The little feller's only trying to be friendly."

"Yeah, well, he can go and be friendly somewhere else," said Bro. "I'm freezing here."

"You know you could try shifting yourself, if you want to catch a few more rays?" said Dude.

Bro chuckled. "Very funny, Dude. Very funny."

And with that, Bro began chowing down on the eucalyptus branch, gradually stripping it of its succulent green leaves. And boy, did those leaves taste good! There were over six hundred kinds of eucalyptus trees in Australia – and this one was a real beaut! One of Bro's faves, in fact.

The more Bro chewed, the heavier his eyelids began to get. The heavier Bro's eyelids got, the less he chewed. The next thing he knew – or rather, the next thing he *didn't* know – Bro had fallen fast asleep.

"SQUAWK! SQUAWK! SQUAWK!" went the sulphur-crested cockatoo in the neighbouring tree.

"Aaaaaaaaagh!" screamed Bro, waking with a start and very nearly falling out of *his* tree.

Squirt laughed. It was the funniest thing he'd seen since the duck-billed platypus had got hiccups.

"Are you still here?" grumbled Bro. "I thought I told you to sling your hook!"

"I'm bored," said Squirt.

Bro thought for a moment. "Bored, eh?"

Squirt nodded.

"See that jumped-up budgie over there?"

Squirt looked where Bro was looking. "The sulphur-crested cockatoo, you mean?"

"Yeah," said Bro. "Bet you can't sneak up and nab one of its tail feathers before I count to a hundred."

"A hundred?" said Squirt.

Bro nodded.

"Bet you I can."

"Three... two... one... go!" said Bro.

Squirt was gone in a flash, finally leaving

Dude and Bro in peace once again, wedged between branches high above The Acacia Koala Sanctuary.

"Heh-heh-heh," chuckled Bro.

"Heh-heh-heh," chuckled Dude. "Genius, mate. Pure genius."

For a while, the only sound to be heard was the sound of Bro chomping contentedly on his eucalyptus branch as the sun rose higher and higher in the cloudless sky.

Suddenly Dude furrowed his brow. Or at least, he furrowed his brow as best a koala could. "Er, Bro?" he said. "Aren't you s'posed to be counting up to a hundred?"

But there was no reply. Bro had fallen fast asleep.

"Heh-heh-heh," chuckled Dude, who was feeling in need of a kip himself. All that chilling had worn him out.

"SQUAWK! SQUAWK! SQUAWK!" went the sulphur-crested cockatoo in the neighbouring tree.

"Aaaaaaaaaaagh!" screamed Dude and Bro, together.

A few seconds later, Squirt appeared – breathless from climbing back up the trunk in double-quick time, but triumphant nevertheless.

"I did it! I did it!" he cried, clutching a brilliant white feather in one of his paws.

"Heh-heh-heh," chuckled Dude. "You did, didn't you? Good on yer, Squirt!"

Bro shook his head in disbelief, but couldn't help chuckling too.

What with all the squawking and all the chuckling, no one noticed Mrs M suddenly appear in the treetop.

"What's going on?" she said.

"Nothing, Ma," said Bro.

"Hello, Dude," said Mrs M.

"G'day, Mrs M," said Dude. "Still no sign of the joey then?"

"Any day now," smiled Mrs M, patting her pouch. "Any day now."

"I reckon it's going to be a girl," said Dude.

"Do you, now?" said Mrs M.

"I reckon it's gonna be annoying," said Bro. "Even *more* annoying than Squirt."

"Hello, Squirty-Wirty," said Mrs M. "Didn't see you there!"

"Maaaaaa!" said Squirt through gritted teeth. "I've told you not to call me that!"

"Aw, have you?" squeaked Mrs M. "Come to Mumsy-Wumsy for a cuddly-wuddly!"

"No!" said Squirt. "Don't want to!"

"Heh-heh-heh," chuckled Bro.

"Heh-heh-heh," chuckled Dude.

Squirt was embarrassed. His mum calling him Squirty-Wirty was bad enough – but doing it in front of Dude and Bro was even worse! It was a good job koalas couldn't blush.

It's not fair, thought Squirt. He'd brought his brother a eucalyptus branch. He'd nabbed a feather from the sulphur-crested cockatoo. And *still* they were making fun of him! When were they going to stop treating him like a baby?

"Come on, boys," said Mrs M. "Time to go."

Dude and Bro immediately stopped chuckling.

"Go?" said Bro. "Go where?"

"The big zoo!" said Mrs M. "Remember?"

Bro looked at Dude, then at Mrs M. He clearly *hadn't* remembered. Neither had Squirt.

"We're all going to the big zoo on the other side of the city!" said Mrs M.

"All of us?" said Squirt.

"Just us koalas," said Mrs M.

"How long for?" said Squirt.

"A month," said Mrs M. "Think of it as a holiday!"

Squirt thought for a moment. A holiday? That sounded like fun! A lot of the folk that came to the sanctuary came because they were on holiday. But he'd never had one before. He'd never been anywhere else before. He'd lived his whole life here. There was a big world out there waiting to be discovered – and Squirt couldn't wait to discover it.

"Cool!" said Squirt.

"Not cool," said Bro.

"What?" said Squirt.

"Not cool at all," said Bro. "Most *un*cool. Isn't that right, Dude?"

"What's that, Bro?" said Dude.

"Why can't we just stay here?" said Bro,

stifling a massive yawn. "We've got trees to chill in… All the eucy branches we can eat… There's no *need* to go anywhere else!"

"Well, we're going, whether you like it or not," said Mrs M. "Now hurry up or we'll miss the truck."

"Whoa! A truck?" said Squirt excitedly. "Cool!"

Bro shot Squirt a glance. "Not cool."

Squirt thought for a moment. "Erm. Guess you're right. It's not *that* cool."

"Come on," said Mrs M.

"In a minute, Ma," said Bro. "There's something me and Dude need to do first."

Dude did his best to furrow his brow again. "There is?"

"We need to see a man about a dingo," said Bro.

"We do?" said Dude.

Bro glared at Dude and nodded furiously. "Yeah, we do!"

"Ohhhhh. Yeah, we do," said Dude. "We definitely do need to see a man about a dingo."

"Well, don't be long," said Mrs M. "The truck's leaving soon. You don't want to miss it."

"Wanna bet?" muttered Bro.

"Come on, Squirty-Wirty!" said Mrs M, beginning to climb back down the tree.

Squirt didn't even notice his mum calling him Squirty-Wirty. He was busy thinking.

Going on holiday to the big zoo sounded cool. But seeing a man about a dingo with his big brother and his big brother's friend sounded pretty cool too.

"I'll just be a minute, Ma!" called Squirt as Mrs M disappeared from view.

Bro stared at Squirt. "What do you think you're doing?"

"I'm coming with you!" grinned Squirt.

"Where to?" said Bro.

"To see a man about a dingo!"

Dude and Bro turned to each other.

"Heh-heh-heh," chuckled Bro.

"Heh-heh-heh," chuckled Dude.

"Why are you laughing?" said Squirt.

"We're not *really* going to see a man

about a dingo, ya dingo!" said Bro.

"You're not?" said Squirt, sounding disappointed.

"It's just an expression!"

"But…" began Squirt.

"But nothing," said Bro. "We're just going to grab a quick forty winks before the truck goes. Isn't that right, mate?"

"Totally, mate," said Dude, stifling a yawn.

Yawns are very catching and before he knew it, Squirt was yawning too. He didn't *want* to feel sleepy. There was *far* too much happening. There was *much* too much excitement in the air! But, well – it wouldn't hurt if he closed his eyes for just a *few* minutes, would it? *No*, thought Squirt. *It wouldn't*. And that's exactly what he did.

Chapter Two

"G'day, mate," said Bro, yawning and rubbing his eyes. "Reckon we must've dropped off for a minute there." There was no reply from Dude. Dude was still fast asleep.

Bro stretched his arms. After eating

eucalyptus leaves, catching rays and sleeping, stretching was one of Bro's favourite things in the whole wide world. Well – in The Acacia Koala Sanctuary anyway.

"Aw, yeah, that's truly magnificent, mate," said Bro. "You know something? I could stretch for miles if I didn't have to come back afterwards."

There was still no reply from Dude. Dude was *still* fast asleep.

Bro cranked open an eye. The sun was high in the sky. Much higher than it had been the last time he'd looked. Maybe they'd dropped off for a bit longer than a minute.

"Wake up! Wake up!" squeaked Squirt, suddenly appearing in the treetop.

"Whoa, calm down, ya wallaby," said Bro. "I'm already awake!"

"Dude's not!" said Squirt, jumping up and down on Dude's tummy and tugging his ears. "Wake up, Dude! Wake up!"

"Uh? What?" said Dude, finally beginning to stir.

"You were sleeping!" said Squirt.

"I was?" said Dude, stifling a yawn. "Oh, right, I was. I was having this really weird dream too."

"Oh, yeah?" said Bro.

"Yeah," said Dude. "Dreamt I was a trampoline."

Bro was puzzled. "You mean, you were *on* a trampoline?"

"No," said Dude. "I dreamt I *was* a trampoline."

"That was me jumping up and down on your tummy!" said Squirt.

"Heh-heh-heh," chuckled Bro.

Dude looked at Squirt. "What d'ya do that for?"

"To wake you up!" said Squirt. "We all fell asleep!"

Dude and Bro turned to each other and shrugged.

"What's the problem?" said Bro.

"We weren't *supposed* to!" said Squirt.

"We weren't?" said Dude.

"They've all gone!" said Squirt, beginning to get more and more agitated.

Dude was beginning to get more and more puzzled. "Who's gone?"

"Ma! Pa! Everyone!"

"Ohhhh!" said Bro. "You mean…"

Squirt nodded vigorously. "All the other

koalas! We missed the truck to the big zoo! It's nearly lunchtime!"

"Nearly lunchtime?" said Dude, suddenly perking up. "Excellent!"

"It's not excellent!" said Squirt. "It's… it's… it's… whatever the opposite of excellent is!"

"*Un*excellent?" suggested Dude.

"Yes! Exactly. So what are we gonna do?" said Squirt, looking at his big brother.

Bro thought for a moment. But only a moment. "Chillax, Squirt. Let's all just catch a few rays. Everything will be cool."

"Chillax?" said Squirt, getting more and more agitated. "How am I supposed to chillax? We've missed the truck! We were supposed to be going to the big zoo! We've been left behind!"

"I totally hear what you're saying, mini-dude," said Dude, helping himself to a eucalyptus branch. "But d'ya reckon this can wait till after lunch?"

"No, it can *not* wait till after lunch!" squeaked Squirt. "We've got to do something! Now!"

"*Do* something?" said Bro, utterly horrified.

"Whoa," said Dude.

"Are you serious?" said Bro.

"Of course I'm serious!" said Squirt. "Ma and Pa are going to be worried sick! And Ma's having a baby, remember?"

"Aw, yeah," said Dude. "The little feller's

right. Your ma's having a joey any time now, Bro."

"I know that!" snapped Bro.

"I know you know that, Bro," said Dude. "I was just saying…"

"Well, don't, Dude," said Bro.

"Stop arguing, you two!" said Squirt, acting more like a big brother than a little one.

"Yeah, Dude," said Bro. "Stop arguing."

"No, you stop arguing, Bro," said Dude.

"No, *you* stop arguing, Dude," said Bro.

"BOTH OF YOU STOP ARGUING!" yelled Squirt.

"Cool," said Dude and Bro, together.

Squirt sighed and gave himself a scratch.

Scratching was good. Not only did it feel nice, but it also helped Squirt to think. And boy, did Squirt need to think!

By now the sun had risen even higher in the cloudless blue sky. Below, visitors were beginning to tuck into picnics, seemingly unconcerned by the lack of koalas. Luckily, there was much more to The Acacia Koala Sanctuary than just koalas. There were kangaroos and wallabies, platypus and wombats, dingoes, snakes, crocodiles, Tasmanian devils – and not forgetting some extremely noisy birds!

"SQUAWK! SQUAWK! SQUAWK!" went the sulphur-crested cockatoo.

"Put a sock in it, beaky!" cried Bro.

"Yeah, some of us are trying to sleep here," said Dude.

Squirt glared at Dude.

"Not me, obviously," said Dude quickly.

"SQUAWK!" went the sulphur-crested cockatoo again, clearly getting very excited about something it had seen.

Squirt looked down and straightaway saw what it was. The buggy was on its way. The buggy full of food.

"It's the keeper!" said Squirt excitedly.

"So?" said Bro.

"We should turn ourselves in!" said Squirt.

"What?" said Bro.

"We have to go down there," said Squirt,

37

disappearing. "Let him see we're still here."

"The little feller's right, Bro," said Dude, getting up and following. "Think about your ma and pa. Think about the joey."

Bro sighed. "All right, all right. I'm coming."

By the time they all reached the ground, the buggy had stopped in order for the keeper to feed the Tasmanian devil. And it looked like the keeper had a helper.

"Can I drive the buggy, Dad?" said a young girl. "Can I, can I, can I?"

"Not now," said the keeper. "We've got work to do."

"Pleeeeeeeeease?" pleaded the girl. "You said it's so easy a koala could do it!"

"Did I really say that?" laughed the keeper.

"Yes!" said the girl. "Press green to go and red to stop, right?"

"That's right. But not now!" said the keeper, grabbing a bucket from the back of the buggy and heading towards an enclosure. "Now, are you going to help me feed these tazzies, or not?"

"OK, OK," said the girl, trudging slowly after her dad.

"Let's go!" said Squirt, scurrying towards the buggy.

Dude and Bro looked at each other for a second before scurrying after him. By the time the keeper and his daughter returned, all three were seated in the back.

"Well, well, well," said the keeper. "What have we got here?"

"Koala bears?" said the girl, sounding surprised.

"We're not bears!" hissed Bro under his breath.

"Shhhh!" said Squirt.

"But I thought they'd all gone, Dad?" said the girl.

"So did I," said the keeper. "Lazy little critters must've slept through their transfer!"

"Aw, they're so cute!" said the girl. "Looks like they're trying to hitch a lift!"

"Well, they can't get a lift in this thing!" said the keeper.

The girl looked disappointed. "Aw, Dad. Why not? It'll be fun!"

"You can't drive a little buggy like this across town!" said the keeper, clapping his hands. "Be far too dangerous! Come on, fellers! Out you get now!"

Dude, Bro and Squirt climbed reluctantly out of the buggy again.

"Bye bye, bears!" called the girl as she and her father climbed back into the buggy and drove off.

"We're not *bears*!" hissed Bro, glaring after them. "We're *koalas*!"

"You tell 'em, mate," said Dude.

"How would *they* like it if we called them human *bears*?" said Bro.

"Heh-heh-heh," chuckled Dude. "Human bears. That's funny, Bro."

Squirt glared at Dude until he stopped chuckling.

"Sorry, mini-dude," said Dude, sheepishly.

But Squirt said nothing. He was too busy

thinking. If they weren't going to get a lift to the big zoo in the buggy, how *were* they going to get there?

Chapter Three

Back in the tree, Squirt watched and scratched. Below, The Acacia Koala Sanctuary was gradually getting busier and busier. Camera-wielding tourists mingled with parties of excited school children. Young couples pushed prams. Toddlers toddled. Siblings squabbled. Elderly folk sat on benches, perfectly happy to watch the world go by.

But Squirt wasn't bothered about any of that. All Squirt was bothered about was where the big zoo was. And how they were going to get there. He knew that it was somewhere on the other side of the city. But how far? And which way?

Squirt gave himself an extra good scratch and suddenly had an idea. If he climbed even higher he might get a better view.

Squirt began scrambling up the tree. As he climbed higher and higher, the branches gradually got thinner and thinner and bendier and bendier. He'd never been this high before. But still Squirt kept on climbing and climbing – only stopping when he got to the very top of the tree. Then, clinging more tightly to a branch than he'd ever clung before, he peered into the distance.

The city was truly enormous! Squirt knew it was big – but he didn't know it was quite *that* big! Buildings rocketed into the air as far as the eye could see. Beyond the buildings Squirt could see green hills. And, in a gap between the hills, Squirt could just make out a splash of blue. The ocean! It had to be the ocean! Squirt had never seen the ocean before, but his mum and dad had told him about it. They'd never seen

the ocean before either. But *their* mas and pas had. Because Squirt's ma and pa's mas and pas had once lived in the forests. The forests beyond the city. Somewhere out there, in the big, wide world.

Squirt sighed. It *had* been a good idea to climb to the top of the tree. The view really *was* amazing. The one thing he couldn't see though, was the big zoo.

A breeze suddenly ruffled the fur on Squirt's ears. The branch began to sway very slightly. But that was enough for Squirt, who immediately started climbing back down through the branches just as fast as he could. If there was one place he didn't want to be when it got windy, it was the very top of a tree!

"Come on, you guys!" said Squirt as he passed Dude and Bro on his way down.

"Uh, what?" said Bro, cranking open an eye. "What's happening?"

"What's happening?" said Squirt, scarcely able to believe his ears. "We're going to the big zoo, remember?"

"We are?" said Bro, stifling a yawn.

"Aw, no," said Dude, stifling an even bigger yawn. "We must've dropped off again, Bro."

"Guess so, Dude," said Bro. "Pass me a eucy branch, will ya? I've fair worked up an appetite having that kip."

"No time for that, Bro," said Dude.

"Look, the little feller's gone and gone."

"Uh?" said Bro. "What do you mean, he's gone and gone, Dude?"

"Squirt," said Dude. "He's gone and gone, Bro."

Bro looked. His friend was right. Squirt *had* gone and gone.

***

By the time Dude and Bro caught up with him, Squirt was halfway across the sanctuary.

"Whoa! Slow down, will ya?" panted Bro.

"Totally," wheezed Dude. "Where's the fire, mini-dude?"

Squirt was puzzled. "Fire? What fire?"

"It's an *expression*," said Bro. "He means,

what's the emergency?"

"Oh, I see," said Squirt, showing no sign of slowing down. As far as he was concerned, it *was* an emergency! "I thought we could ask someone."

"Ask someone what?" said Bro.

"Where the big zoo is!" said Squirt.

"Cool," said Dude, stifling a yawn. "Then maybe we can catch a few more rays."

"We most certainly cannot!" said Squirt. "Once we find out *where* the big zoo is, we can think about how we're going to get there!"

"*Then* we can catch a few more rays?" said Dude hopefully.

Squirt sighed with exasperation. "No!

Then we *go* there!"

"Heh-heh-heh," chuckled Bro.

"Dunno what you're laughing about, Bro," said Dude.

Bro thought for a moment. *He* didn't know what he was laughing about either.

By now they'd reached the aviary – an enormous enclosure full of brightly-coloured birds, whooping and swooping about. Not only was it a very popular part of The Acacia Koala Sanctuary – it was by far the noisiest!

Sat on a branch, bobbing up and down, was a bright green parrot all by itself.

"Excuse me?" said Squirt, struggling to make himself heard above the hullabaloo.

"Excuse me?" said the parrot.

"Do you know where the big zoo is?" said Squirt.

"Do you know where the big zoo is?" said the parrot.

"No, I asked you first," said Squirt.

"No, I asked you first," said the parrot.

"Heh-heh-heh," chuckled Bro.

"Heh-heh-heh," chuckled Dude.

"Heh-heh-heh," chuckled the parrot.

But Squirt wasn't amused. Squirt was *far* from amused. "Are you going to copy me all day?"

"Are you going to copy me all day?" said the parrot.

"Cool," said Bro.

"Cool," said the parrot.

Dude beckoned to Bro to come closer, and whispered in his ear so that the parrot couldn't hear him. "Say something rude, Bro! See if it copies that too!"

Bro burst out laughing. Not only because it was a funny idea, but because he had unbelievably tickly ears.

"Stop, Dude!" screeched Bro. "I can't stand it!"

"Stop, Dude!" screeched the parrot. "I can't stand it!"

"Oh, this is ridiculous!" said Squirt,

storming off.

"Oh, this is ridiculous!" said the parrot.

"Heh-heh-heh," chuckled Bro, following Squirt.

"Heh-heh-heh," chuckled Dude, following Bro.

"Heh-heh-heh," chuckled the parrot, watching all three of them go.

***

Next to the aviary was a big pool. A big pool with a wall around it. It wasn't a terribly high wall though. It was certainly no match for a koala. In next to no time, Dude, Bro and Squirt had all climbed up one side and down the other.

"Who's coming for a paddle?" said Bro,

heading straight for the water.

"Aw, yeah. Defo, mate," said Dude. "Could do with cooling down."

But Squirt wasn't so sure. He'd spotted a couple of bulging eyes poking up through the water. And they didn't look particularly friendly either.

"Aw, cool, look," said Bro, reaching the

water and also spotting the eyes. "A frog!"

Dude looked. "Some size of frog, mate."

"What do you mean?" said Bro.

"Those eyes are awfully far apart."

"Don't be silly, mate!" laughed Bro, paddling towards the eyes and holding out a paw. "Here, froggy! Here, froggy-woggy!"

"I don't think you should…" began Squirt.

But before Squirt could finish, there was a sudden watery gurgling sound as, from beneath the surface of the water, a huge shape gradually began to appear.

Dude and Bro stood frozen in the pool as they came face to face with a huge crocodile. And it didn't look happy.

"G'day, mate," said Bro. He didn't know much about crocs. He wasn't sure he wanted to either.

"So," said the croc, in a big, booming voice. "You thought I was a frog, did you?"

"Heh-heh-heh," chuckled Bro nervously. "No offence, mate."

"Heh-heh-heh," chuckled Dude, equally nervously.

There was an awkward silence as the two paddling koalas looked at the croc – and the croc looked at the two paddling koalas. Bro thought he'd better say something. Anything. Anything at all.

"Don't suppose you know where I can get my paws on a nice juicy eucy branch, do ya, sport?"

Dude looked at Bro in disbelief. "What did you say *that* for, Bro?"

"A *what?*" boomed the croc.

"Erm, a eucalyptus branch?" said Bro, slightly hesitantly.

The croc snarled, baring more teeth

than Dude and Bro had ever seen in a single mouth before. "Do I *look* like I eat *eucalyptus?*"

"Mate, you look like you eat just about *anything!*" said Bro.

"What?" boomed the crocodile.

"I think there's been a slight misunderstanding," said Squirt, deciding it was time to step in.

"Oh, you do, do you?" said the crocodile.

"Yes," said Squirt. "Actually, what we were wondering was, do you happen to know where the big zoo is?"

"The big zoo?" said the crocodile.

"Yes, you see that's where all the other koalas have been taken. That's why we're trying to get there!"

"So *that's* what you are," said the crocodile. "Koalas."

Bro had a sudden thought. "You don't happen to *eat* koalas by any chance, do ya?"

"I'm not sure," grinned the croc. "I've never actually tried one. Yet."

"Yet?" gulped Bro.

"Erm, Bro, I reckon we should probably get going," said Dude.

"Er, yeah," said Bro. "Reckon you're right there, Dude."

"Must you?" said the croc. "That's a pity."

"Yeah, well, we've gotta see a man about a dingo," said Dude. "Isn't that right, Bro?"

"Yeah, defo, Dude. A dingo."

But by now it was too late. The croc had already opened its jaws wide to reveal even *more* teeth than before! More than enough to make mincemeat of a couple of koalas. And by the look of things, that was precisely what it was about to do.

"It's been nice knowing you, Bro," said Dude.

"Been a pleasure, Dude," said Bro.

The croc glanced from Bro to Dude, then back to Bro again, as if it was trying to make up its mind who to eat first. Which one was going to be the starter and which one was going to be the main course?

But before it could make up its mind, Squirt suddenly jumped on to the croc's back and ran all the way up – from the tip of its knobbly tail, to the top of its leathery head.

Dude and Bro were amazed. They were even *more* amazed when the croc suddenly burst out giggling hysterically.

"Stop, stop, stop! That tickles!"

"Run for it!" yelled Squirt.

Dude and Bro didn't need telling twice. They ran for it!

"See you later, alligator!" said Bro.

Squirt jumped up in the air, before bouncing off the croc's snout like it was a springboard in a swimming pool.

Boing!!!

"In a while, crocodile!" yelled Squirt, flying through the air before landing on the ground, climbing back over the wall and scurrying after the other two just as fast as he could.

Chapter Four

It wasn't difficult for Squirt to catch up with Dude and Bro. They'd both collapsed in a heap under the nearest tree.

"I'm fair tuckered out, mate," panted Bro.

"Me too, Bro," panted Dude.

"Thought we were both goners back there," panted Bro.

"Me too, Bro," panted Dude.

"Thought we were on our way to that great eucy tree in the sky," panted Bro.

"Me too, Bro," panted Dude.

"You're welcome," said Squirt, plonking himself down next to them.

"Uh?" said Bro. "What for?

"What for?" said Squirt. "For saving your lives!"

Dude and Bro looked at each other as if it hadn't even crossed their minds that if it hadn't been for Squirt they may *well* have been on their way to that great eucalyptus tree in the sky by now.

"He's right, Bro," said Dude. "He did."

"S'pose," said Bro grumpily, with a barely noticeable shrug of his shoulders.

But if either Dude or Bro was thinking of thanking Squirt, there was no time, because at that moment the air was suddenly filled with the sound of raucous, ringing laughter.

"Wah, ha, ha, ha, ha!" said a shrill voice from above. "That was the funniest thing I've *ever* seen!"

The three koalas looked up. There, sitting in a branch, was a kookaburra.

"Who are you?" said Squirt.

"The name's Kylie," said the kookaburra, before bursting out laughing again. "Seriously, I've seen some funny things –

but *that* takes the biscuit!"

Bro wasn't happy. Not only had he and Dude just narrowly avoided becoming koala Bolognese, but now some feathered joker was poking fun at him.

"Do you mind?" said Bro.

"No," said Kylie, barely able to contain herself. "I don't mind at all!"

And with that, Kylie the kookaburra burst out laughing again – this time even louder and longer.

Bro, meanwhile, was getting crosser and crosser.

"You don't think that was funny then?" said Kylie.

"Certainly don't, mate," said Bro. "That

croc had more teeth than I've had eucy branches! And let me tell you – I've had a fair few eucy branches in my time!"

"Wah, ha, ha, ha, ha!" said Kylie. "Seriously?"

"Seriously," said Bro.

"The way the little guy ran up its back and bounced off its hooter like that?"

Bro remained stony-faced.

"You're right," said Kylie. "That wasn't funny. It was *hilarious*!"

There was a moment's pause before Kylie burst out laughing *so* loud, and *so* long, she very nearly toppled off her branch.

That did it. Squirt started to laugh too.

And when Squirt started to laugh, Dude started to laugh as well.

"She's right, Bro," said Dude. "It *was* pretty funny, come to think of it."

"Speak for yourself, mate," said Bro. But it was no good. He'd already begun to grin. He didn't want to. He was still unhappy about Kylie making fun of him. But in the end he just couldn't help it. The crazy kookaburra's laughter was catching. Any second now, he was going to burst out laughing too. He could feel it building up inside, like a sneeze. There was only thing for it. He was going to have to let it out.

"Ha, ha, ha, ha, ha!!!" laughed Bro.

"Ha, ha, ha, ha, ha!!!" laughed Dude.

"Ha, ha, ha, ha, ha!!!" laughed Squirt.

"HA, HA, HA, HA, HA!" said Kylie.

"Stop!" yelled Squirt, suddenly coming to his senses.

Everybody was so surprised that they immediately stopped laughing too. Even Kylie.

"Haven't you forgotten something?" said Squirt to Dude and Bro.

Dude and Bro looked at each other and shrugged.

"Can't remember, mate," said Dude.

"You can't remember if you've forgotten something?" said Kylie. "Now *that's* funny!"

"No, it's not," said Squirt sternly. "It's not funny at all!"

"It's not?" said Kylie.

"We're trying to find our way to the big zoo," said Squirt.

"The big zoo, eh?" said Kylie.

Squirt nodded. "On the other side of the city."

"I see," said Kylie.

"I don't suppose you know how to get there, do you?" said Squirt, hopefully.

"Funny you should say that," said Kylie.

"You do?" squeaked Squirt excitedly. "Really?"

"Nah, not really," said Kylie. "That's why it's funny!"

There was the briefest of pauses before Kylie, Dude and Bro all burst out laughing again.

Squirt sighed. For a moment he'd actually thought that Kylie was about to offer some sensible advice. For a moment he'd actually thought she really *did* know how to get to the big zoo. But now it seemed that she didn't. She was just joking.

"Is there anything you *don't* find funny?" said Squirt.

"As a matter of fact, there *is* one thing," said Kylie.

"What's that?" said Squirt.

"Bananas," said Kylie.

"Bananas?" said Squirt. "You don't find *bananas* funny?"

Kylie looked at Squirt for a split second before suddenly bursting out laughing again. "Just joking!" she said. "Bananas are the funniest things ever!"

"Ha, ha, ha, ha, ha!!!" laughed Bro.

"Ha, ha, ha, ha, ha!!!" laughed Dude.

"Oh, this is driving me round the bend!" said Squirt.

"That's it!" cried Kylie.

"That's what?" said Squirt.

"*That's* where the big zoo is!" said Kylie. "Round the bend!"

Squirt eyed Kylie suspiciously. "Really?"

"Really," said Kylie.

"You're not joking?" said Squirt.

"Defo," said Kylie. "Not joking!"

Things were looking up, thought Squirt. The big zoo was round the bend! It was a start. But there was one more question.

"Which bend?"

"What's that?" said Kylie.

"Which bend is the big zoo around?" said Squirt.

"I've no idea!" said Kylie, before bursting out laughing again.

Dude and Bro burst out laughing again

too, even though they knew they probably shouldn't. They just couldn't help it.

"Quiet, you two!" said Squirt. "I'm trying to think here!"

"Sorry, Squirt," said Bro.

"Yeah, totally sorry, mini-dude," said Dude.

Squirt gave himself a scratch and looked around. He hadn't noticed before, but they were actually very close to a gateway in the main wall – the wall that ran all the way round the sanctuary. Not only that, but the gate was wide open! And not only *that*, but parked by the open gateway was a keeper's buggy. The same keeper's buggy they'd seen earlier. And the keeper was nowhere to be seen. It was almost too good to be true.

"Come on, guys!" said Squirt, setting off immediately.

"Where are you going?" said Bro.

"Round the bend!" cried Squirt. "You coming, or what?"

Dude and Bro looked at each other for a second before setting off after Squirt. By the time they caught up with him he was already standing on the driver's seat, studying the controls.

"Now, let me see," he said. "What was it again? Press green to go and red to stop?"

"What are you doing?" said Bro.

"What does it *look* like I'm doing?" said

Squirt. "We need to get to the big zoo somehow!"

"But…" said Bro.

"But what?" said Squirt. "You're not scared, are you?"

"No!" said Bro quickly. "You can't just take it, that's all."

Squirt turned to face his big brother. "Do you have any better ideas?"

"As a matter of fact, I do," said Bro. "We could go back to our own tree, chow down on a couple of eucy branches and catch a few rays."

Bro looked at Dude, expecting him to chuckle. But Dude didn't chuckle.

"The little feller's right, mate. We need

to get there *somehow*."

Dude hopped up into the buggy to join Squirt, leaving Bro alone on the ground.

Bro looked around anxiously. He'd heard voices. Human voices. And they were getting louder.

"Look, Dad!" said the keeper's daughter, spotting the buggy and scarcely believing what she was seeing.

But the keeper was too busy talking on his phone to pay any attention to his daughter, or to see Bro scramble up to join Squirt and Dude.

"So easy a koala could do it, eh?" said Squirt. "We'll soon see about that then, won't we?"

"Dad! Dad! Look!" said the girl, frantically tugging at the keeper's sleeve. But the keeper just kept talking on his phone without so much as a glance at the buggy.

"Hurry up, mate!" said Dude, looking back anxiously.

"DAAAAD!" shouted the girl, finally getting her dad's attention.

"Can't you see I'm on the phone here?" said the keeper angrily.

At that moment, Squirt stretched forward and pressed the green button. All of a sudden, the buggy lurched forward and started to move! The keeper was still busy talking on the phone. His daughter could still hardly believe her eyes as Dude, Bro and Squirt headed for the gate.

They were off!

Chapter Five

The buggy whizzed out of The Acacia Koala Sanctuary and down a long, tree-lined driveway. Squirt was behind the wheel, Dude and Bro sat beside him on the front seat.

"Whoa, this is amazing!" cried Dude, his

ears flapping furiously in the breeze. "Don't you reckon, Bro?"

Bro said nothing.

"Bro?" said Dude, giving his friend a nudge. "Isn't this totally awesome?"

"Yeah, sure, Dude," said Bro unconvincingly. "Totally awesome, mate."

"Looks like they were right!" grinned Squirt. "A koala really *can* drive one of these things! It's easy-peasy!"

"Heh-heh-heh," chuckled Dude. "Cheesy-squeezy!"

"Not cheesy-squeezy!" laughed Squirt. "Easy-peasy!"

"Heh-heh-heh," chuckled Dude. "Breezy-queasy!"

"No!" laughed Squirt. "Not breezy-queasy! Easy-peasy!"

"Heh-heh-heh," chuckled Dude.

But still Bro said nothing. His eyes were fixed firmly on the road ahead. He could see something that the other two couldn't.

"You OK, Bro?" said Dude.

"Look out!" said Bro.

"What's that, Bro?" yelled Dude. "You'll have to speak up!"

"Look out!" said Bro, a bit louder.

"Nah, sorry, Bro. Still can't hear ya!" yelled Dude. "What's that you're saying?"

"LOOK OUT!!!" screamed Bro at the top of his voice, as the buggy finally reached the end of the tree-lined driveway and shot straight out into a big, wide road, with traffic screaming past in either direction.

"Aaaaaaagh!" screamed Squirt as a bus whizzed past one way.

"Aaaaaaagh!" screamed Dude as a car zoomed past the other way.

"AAAAAAAGH!" screamed Bro.

"A A A A A A A A A A A A A A G H ! ! !" screamed all three koalas together.

Squirt tried to remember which button was which. Which was stop and which was go? Red or green? Green or red? But in the heat of the moment, he couldn't think clearly. He desperately wanted to scratch – but he knew that was the *last* thing he should do. No matter what, he just *had* to

keep his paws on the wheel! There was
only one thing for it, thought Squirt. He
was going to have to just keep going and
hope for the best!

There was an almighty roar as a
motorbike suddenly shot by. The rider
shouted something, but whatever it was was
drowned out by the sound of a horn being

furiously tooted as another car narrowly
avoided the buggy.

"Gotta keep going! Gotta keep going!"
said Squirt to himself, as a truck driver
stared in disbelief, swerving at the last
minute and just avoiding them.

"Gotta keep going! Gotta keep going!"
said Squirt again, as a cyclist skidded and

almost crashed into a lamp post.

And then, all of a sudden, it was over. Miraculously, they'd somehow made it to the other side of the road. There was a slight bump as the buggy mounted the pavement.

"Mind how ya go, Squirt," muttered Bro.

"Excuse me?" said Squirt, indignantly.

"Drive a bit more carefully, will ya?" said Bro.

"A bit more carefully?" squeaked Squirt. He couldn't believe his ears. He'd single-handedly negotiated the road and avoided all the traffic. And this was all the thanks he got?

"Nice one, mini-dude," said Dude, as if he'd read Squirt's mind. "That was a pretty close call back there."

"You're welcome, *Dude*," said Squirt pointedly.

"Which way now?" said Dude.

Squirt didn't reply. He was concentrating on driving along the pavement.

"What do you mean, which way, Dude?" said Bro. "Which way where?"

"Where do you think?" said Squirt.

"I've no idea," said Bro. "Where *do* you think?"

"Heh-heh-heh," chuckled Dude.

"Which way to the big zoo!" said Squirt.

"Oh, right," said Bro. "I've no idea."

"Me neither," said Dude. "That's why I asked."

Squirt sighed. Trying to get sense out of Dude and Bro was like trying to get juice out of a shrivelled up eucalyptus leaf: just about impossible.

There was a sudden tooting sound behind them on the pavement. Dude and Bro swivelled round to see what it was. Squirt looked in the rear-view mirror. He didn't dare turn round for fear of crashing into something or someone.

An old man was trying to overtake them on a mobility scooter. The kind of scooter used by folk who couldn't easily walk by themselves. Wherever he was going, he seemed in an awful hurry to get there.

"Whoa! Will you look at that!" said Bro.

"Awesome," said Dude.

"D'ya reckon he's trying to race us, Dude?" said Bro.

"Heh-heh-heh," chuckled Dude. "Looks like it, Bro."

"Cool!" said Bro.

But the old man didn't look cool. In fact, he looked anything *but* cool – and whenever he wasn't busy tooting his horn, he was angrily shaking his fist in the koalas' direction.

"Get out of the way, you kids!" yelled the old man, getting closer and closer. "You're blocking the pavement!"

Squirt *tried* to get out of the way, but whenever he turned the wheel to the right

– the old man turned to the right as well. Whenever Squirt turned to the left – so did the old man.

"Heh-heh-heh," chuckled Bro.

"Heh-heh-heh," chuckled Dude.

They carried on zigzagging down the pavement before the old man eventually managed to overtake as they went round a corner.

"Road hogs!" he yelled, disappearing into the distance and still shaking his fist.

"We're not hogs! We're *koalas*!" said Bro, grumpily.

"Most uncool being overtaken by one of those things," said Dude. "Can't you go any faster, mini-dude?"

But Squirt wasn't listening. He'd spotted something up ahead. "Whoa!"

"What is it?" said Bro.

"Look!" said Squirt.

Dude and Bro both looked. And what they both looked at didn't look good. The old man had stopped his scooter and was talking to somebody. Somebody in a uniform.

"Uh-oh. Are you thinking what I'm thinking, Dude?" said Bro.

"Dunno, Bro," said Dude. "Depends what you're thinking."

"I'm thinking that looks like a policeman, Dude," said Bro. "I'm thinking the old feller's telling him all about us. I'm thinking we could be in a fair bit of trouble here if we're not careful."

"That's exactly what *I'm* thinking," said Squirt. "And I'll tell you something else."

"What?" said Dude and Bro, together.

"We're not going to get close enough to find out!"

"We're not?" said Bro.

"We're not," said Squirt, suddenly turning the steering wheel, sending the buggy careering round another corner and down a side street.

"Where are we going now?" said Bro anxiously.

"Round the bend," chuckled Dude.

But Squirt didn't say anything. Squirt *couldn't* say anything. He was far too busy staring open-mouthed at the sight that greeted them.

A huge removals lorry was parked by the side of the road. Not only that, but the back door was open and the ramp was down. There was no avoiding it. They were

much too close. There was nothing Squirt could do.

"Aaaaaaaaaagh!" screamed Squirt as the buggy zoomed up the ramp.

"Aaaaaaaaaaagh!" screamed Dude.

"Mummy!" yelled Bro. "I mean, AAAAAAAAAAAGH!!!"

The buggy hit something soft and came to an abrupt halt. Everybody breathed a huge sigh of relief. It had been *some* journey. But what now?

"Bro?" said Dude.

"What?" said Bro.

"Did you just say, *Mummy?*"

"No!" said Bro, emphatically.

"Yes, you did," said Dude. "I heard you."

"Shhhhh!" said Squirt. "There's someone coming."

They listened. They could hear footsteps. Then everything suddenly went dark as the door was closed. A moment later there was a deep rumble as the engine burst into life and the truck – along with its three new passengers – set off down the road.

Chapter Six

"Dude?" said Bro, stifling a yawn.

"G'day, Bro," said Dude, stifling an even bigger one.

"Where are ya?" said Bro.

"Right here, Bro," said Dude. "Where are you?"

"I'm right here too, Dude," said Bro.

There was a slight pause.

"So how come I can't see you, Bro?" said Dude.

"Try opening your eyes," said Bro.

"They *are* open," said Dude.

"That's funny, mine are open too, Dude," said Bro. "What's going on?"

"It's dark," said Squirt. "That's what's going on."

"Who are you?" said Bro.

"Squirt?" said Squirt. "Your brother? Remember?"

"Oh, yeah," said Bro. "My annoying little brother. I remember now."

"Heh-heh-heh," chuckled Dude.

"You fell asleep," said Squirt.

"Heh-heh-heh," chuckled Dude again.

"You too, Dude," said Squirt.

"Really?" said Dude, sounding surprised. "Whoa. Don't remember doing that."

"Heh-heh-heh," chuckled Bro.

There was a muffled tooting sound.

"Was that you, Dude?" said Bro.

"Not me, Bro," said Dude. "I thought it was you."

Squirt sighed in the dark. "It was the truck!"

There was another slight pause.

"Truck?" said Dude. "What truck?"

"The one that we're in!" said Squirt getting more and more exasperated.

"We're in a truck?" said Dude.

There was a jolt as the truck pulled up and the engine was switched off. Everything suddenly went very quiet.

"Aw, yeah," said Bro. "I remember now. We're in a buggy. We drove up a ramp!"

"Cool," said Dude.

They could hear footsteps. A moment later the door opened and the inside of the truck was bathed in warm, bright sunlight.

"Aw, ya beauty," said Bro, stretching. "Might just catch a few more rays."

"Me too," said Dude.

"There's no time for that," said Squirt.

"There's *always* time to catch a few more rays!" said Bro.

"Not today, there isn't!" said Squirt. "Come on! Let's go! This truck's not going any further!"

By now the ramp had been lowered and voices could be heard. Human voices. They needed to act – and they needed to act fast.

"Quick! This way!" hissed Squirt, scurrying towards a large cardboard box. He tested the lid. It opened. He scrambled in, before peering back out again. "Hurry up, you guys!"

Dude and Bro glanced at each other before running to the box and diving in head first. Squirt pulled the lid down and once again the three koalas were plunged into darkness.

"C'mon, Stevo," said a muffled voice. "Let's take this one first."

"No worries," said a second muffled voice.

"One, two, three… hup," said the first voice.

Squirt, Dude and Bro suddenly felt themselves being lifted into the air.

"Blimey, Daz," said the second voice. "Don't remember it being quite *this* heavy!"

"Don't remember that buggy being there either, mate," said the first voice.

"Me neither, mate," said the second voice. "I guess Bruce must've loaded it."

"Guess you're right there, mate," said the first voice. "Come on. This thing weighs a ton."

"Heh-heh-heh," chuckled Dude and Bro together.

"Shhhh!" said Squirt.

"Did you hear that?" said one of the voices.

"Let's have a look, shall we?" said the other.

The koalas felt a bump as they were lowered to the ground. A moment later the lid of the box opened and they found themselves face to face with two men.

"Well, well, well," said one of them. "What do we have here?"

"Blow me down," said the other one. "Koala bears!"

"We're *not* bears!" muttered Bro to himself.

"No wonder it was so heavy! What are

we going to do, Daz?"

"Search me, mate."

"Hey, guys!" called a voice. "Come and give me a hand here, will you?"

Daz and Stevo looked at each other and then at the koalas.

"You little fellers stay right where you are," said Daz.

"Coming, Bruce!" called Stevo.

And with that the two men disappeared, leaving the three koalas alone in the truck. The men might not have known what to do, but Squirt, Dude and Bro knew *exactly* what to do.

"Run for it!" yelled Squirt, hopping out of the box and shooting off down the ramp just as fast as he could.

"I'm running for it, Squirt! I'm running for it!" yelled Bro. "Are you running for it, Dude?"

"Totally!" yelled Dude.

"This way!" yelled Squirt, spotting a tree and quickly scrambling up the trunk.

"Right behind you!" yelled Bro, scrambling up the trunk after his little brother.

"What he said!" yelled Dude, scrambling up the trunk after his friend.

The only problem was, it wasn't a very high tree. In fact, it was just one of a series of small trees sprouting out of a pavement at regular intervals. But it at least provided a bit of shelter and allowed the koalas time to catch their breath and think what they were going to do next.

"Grrrrrrrrrrrrrrrrrrr!" growled something below.

Squirt, Bro and Dude looked down to see something hairy and dribbly and not very friendly at all, looking back up at them.

"Woof! Woof! Woof!" said the hairy, dribbly thing.

"Aaaaaaaaaagh!" screamed Bro and Dude, clinging on to each other to stop themselves from falling out of the tree.

"W-w-what are you?" stuttered Squirt.

"What *am* I?" said the hairy, dribbly thing. "What do you mean, what *am* I? I'm

a dog! That's what I am!"

"A dog?" said Squirt.

"Have you never seen a dog before?" said the dog.

"No," said Squirt.

It was true too. Squirt had seen all kinds of animals and birds before, but never a dog. Dogs weren't allowed in The Acacia Koala Sanctuary.

"What are *you*, anyway?" said the dog. "Some kind of bear?"

"We're *not* bears! We're koalas!" said Bro, angrily.

"All right, all right," said the dog. "Keep your fur on!"

"Heh-heh-heh," chuckled Dude.

Bro glared at Dude. "Put a sock in it, ya wallaby!"

"Who are yer mates?" said the dog.

"This is Bro," said Squirt.

"G'day," said Bro, grumpily.

"And this is Dude," said Squirt.

"Totally," said Dude.

"I'm Squirt," said Squirt. "What's your name?"

"Rolf," said the dog.

"Heh-heh-heh," chuckled Bro. "Rolf, Rolf."

"Heh-heh-heh. Rolf, Rolf," chuckled Dude.

"Something funny about that?" said Rolf.

"No, no," said Squirt quickly. "Nothing

funny at all. We're trying to get somewhere and we're lost and, well… it's been a long day and we're all a bit tired. Isn't that right, guys?"

But Dude and Bro weren't paying any attention. For some inexplicable reason they still seemed to think that a dog called Rolf was just about the funniest thing they'd ever heard and were chuckling away to themselves.

"Guys?" said Squirt.

"What?" said Bro.

"I was just saying, it's been a long day and we're all a bit tired?"

"Aw, yeah," said Bro, stretching and stifling a yawn.

"Totally, mate," said Dude, stretching and stifling an even bigger yawn.

"I see," said Rolf. "Where are you trying to get to?"

"The big zoo," said Squirt.

"The big zoo?" said Rolf.

"Yes!" said Squirt, allowing himself to get just ever so slightly excited. "You don't happen to know where it is by any chance, do you?"

"The big zoo?" said Rolf.

Squirt nodded vigorously.

"As a matter of fact, I do," said Rolf.

"Fantastic!" said Squirt. "Where is it?"

"It's…" began Rolf.

"There you are, Rolf!" said a voice at

that precise moment.

Rolf turned his head to see where the voice was coming from.

"Where is it?" said Squirt. "Where's the big zoo, Rolf? Please tell us! Quick!"

"I've been looking *everywhere* for you!" said a woman, appearing under the tree and clipping a lead to Rolf's collar.

"Woof! Woof!" said Rolf, wagging his tail furiously.

"You mustn't run off like that!" said the woman. "One of these days you're going to get yourself lost for good!"

"Woof! Woof!" said Rolf.

"Come on," said the woman, leading Rolf away. "Let's get you home."

"No, wait! Rolf! Come back!" called Squirt from up in the tree. "You can't leave now!"

"Woof!" said Rolf, disappearing into the distance.

"Aaaaaaagh!" said Squirt, watching Rolf go. It was *so* frustrating. He'd been a whisker away from telling them where the big zoo was. How were they going to find out where it was now?

"That is *so* cool," said Bro.

There was nothing cool about the situation as far as Squirt was concerned. "What is?"

"How dogs can wag their tails like that," said Bro.

"Totally, mate," said Dude.

"I wish koalas had got tails," said Bro.

"That would be awesome, Bro," said Dude.

"Real long tails, I mean," said Bro, waggling his bottom. "You can't wag these stumpy little things!"

"Heh-heh-heh," chuckled Dude, waggling his bottom.

Squirt shook his head in disbelief. Of all the things they'd got to worry about just now, not having a decent tail to wag was way, *way* down the list.

"Come on, guys," said Squirt, beginning to climb down the tree.

"Where are you going now, Squirt?" said Bro.

"I don't know," said Squirt. "All I know is that we're not going to get to the big zoo by sitting in a tree waggling our bottoms all day."

Dude and Bro looked at each other for a moment.

"He's right, Bro," said Dude, following Squirt.

"S'pose so," sighed Bro, following Dude.

Chapter Seven

Squirt, Bro and Dude scurried along the pavement, doing their best to keep out of sight of any humans. Their mission was to get to the big zoo – wherever that was. The last thing they needed now was to be caught and taken back to The Acacia

Koala Sanctuary.

"Hurry!" hissed Squirt.

"We're hurrying! We're hurrying!" said Bro.

"Totally," said Dude.

They turned a corner and stopped dead

in their tracks. There in front of them was quite simply the biggest building they'd ever seen. A gigantic shopping mall, glinting in the sun and stretching as far as the eye could see. Hundreds of people were streaming in and out of the main entrance.

The ones going in were empty-handed. The ones coming out were loaded down with bulging carrier bags.

"Whoa, will ya look at that?" said Bro.

"I'm looking, Bro! I'm looking!" said Dude.

"Whoa!" said Squirt, mesmerised by what he saw and temporarily forgetting all about the mission. The mission could wait. For a few seconds, anyway.

They soon found themselves being sucked towards the entrance. They seemed powerless to resist, almost as if the mall was some kind of huge magnet. And then they saw it. An enormous glass window – full of the most amazing, colourful and exciting looking things they'd *ever* seen! They stood transfixed for a few seconds, before Squirt's curiosity eventually got the better of him.

"Come on," he said, weaving in and out of a sea of legs and heading for the doorway.

Dude and Bro didn't need telling twice and followed immediately.

"Just try and stop me," said Bro.

"Totally!" said Dude.

Once safely inside the shop, they stopped again to take in the view. And what a view it was. In one direction, a little track with tiny cars whizzing round and round. In another direction, a model railway with perfect tiny houses and perfect tiny people standing on a station platform. But something else had caught Dude's eye.

"Whoa!"

"What, Dude?" said Bro, turning to see what Dude was looking at.

What Dude was looking at turned out to be a huge pile of soft, furry creatures, all jumbled together. Bears, penguins, kangaroos, ducks, elephants, giraffes – even crocodiles and dinosaurs.

"Let's get outta here!" said Dude.

Bro looked at his friend. "What are you talking about, Dude?"

"I'm not hanging around here, Bro!" said Dude. "Far too dangerous! I'm off!"

"Are you serious?" said Bro.

"Totally!" said Dude.

"They're not *real*," said Bro. "They're toys!"

"Toys?" said Dude.

"You know, like the ones the kids buy from the Sanctuary shop," said Bro.

"Oh, yeah," said Dude, looking a bit more closely.

"Have you ever seen a furry croc before?" said Bro.

"No, Bro," said Dude. "Can't say I have."

"Was the croc that nearly made a koala kebab out of us furry?"

"No, Bro," said Dude. "Can't say he was."

"There you go then," said Bro. "Ya wallaby!"

"Cool! In that case…" said Dude,

immediately running towards the pile and diving in head first.

"Heh-heh-heh! Excellent idea, Dude!" chuckled Bro, doing exactly the same.

"Erm, actually guys, I'm not sure that *is* such an excellent idea," said Squirt, hiding behind a cabinet full of games and jigsaw puzzles. But it was too late. A small girl had already spotted them and was desperate to take a closer look.

"Look, Mummy!" said the small girl, freeing herself from her mother's hand and rushing up to the pile of soft, furry animals – and two very *real* animals.

"What is it, darling?" said the mummy.

"Koala bears!"

"We're *not* bears!" muttered Bro through firmly gritted teeth.

The small girl reached out and tickled Dude's tummy.

"Heh-heh-heh," chuckled Dude.

"Look, Mummy! They giggle!" squealed the small girl in delight, tickling Bro's tummy too.

"Heh-heh-heh," chuckled Bro, despite still being cross.

"That is so neat!" squealed the girl. "Can I have one, Mummy? Can I? Can I? Can I?"

"Not today, darling," said the mummy.

"Pleeeeeeeeeeeeeeease?" pleaded the girl.

"Not *today*!" said the mummy, grabbing

the small girl by the hand and pulling her away. "Another day!"

"That's what you *always* say!" wailed the small girl, turning round to have one last, lingering look.

Bro winked. Dude waved. The small girl opened her mouth in disbelief, but before she could say anything, her mother dragged her away.

"Come on!" hissed Squirt. "Time to go!"

"Aw, do we *have* to?" said Bro.

"Yes, we have to!" said Squirt. "Think about Ma and Pa. They'll be worried sick!"

"Cool!" said Dude.

"What?" said Squirt. "You think my Ma and Pa being worried sick is cool?"

"Uh?" said Dude, distractedly. "No, mini-dude. That's not cool. *They're* cool!"

Squirt and Bro turned round to find Dude staring at a display of masks.

"Cool!" said Bro.

"That's what I said, Bro," said Dude.

"What are we waiting for, Dude?" said Bro.

"There's no time to…" began Squirt. But it was too late. Dude and Bro had already dashed over to the display.

"Heh-heh-heh," chuckled Dude, putting on a monster mask.

"Heh-heh-heh," chuckled Bro, putting on an alien mask.

"Come on, Squirt!" said Bro. "Your turn!"

"But…" began Squirt.

"But what?" said Dude. "Don't be a party pooper!"

Squirt knew that they really should get going. But he didn't want to be a party pooper either.

"You should totally do it, mini-dude!" said Dude.

Squirt grabbed a pirate mask and put it on.

"Heh-heh-heh," chuckled Dude and Bro together.

"OK, kids!" boomed a nearby voice. "Time to go to the zoo!"

The three koalas looked at each other. The zoo?

"Everybody in a line!" said the voice. "Who's not here?"

"I'm not here!" said another voice, prompting a gale of laughter.

"Heh-heh-heh," chuckled Bro. "I'm not here. That's funny, Dude!"

"Heh-heh-heh," chuckled Dude. "I'm not here either, Bro!"

"OK, quiet please, guys!" said the first voice. "I want you all to walk – not run – *walk* to the coach!"

A *coach* to the zoo? Squirt couldn't believe his ears. "Right, come on, you two! Quick!"

"Where to?" said Bro.

"I'll give you a clue," said Squirt. "It begins with *z* and ends in *oo*."

Dude and Bro looked at each other.

"I give up," said Bro.

"Me too," said Dude.

"The *zoo!*" hissed Squirt, dashing off. "We've got to get on that coach before those kids do! Come on!"

Dude and Bro dashed after Squirt,

eventually catching up just as he reached the exit.

As they ran back through the doors of the toy shop and into the mall, a high-pitched electronic alarm suddenly went off.

"Whoa. Sounds like someone's in trouble!" said Dude.

"Yes," said Squirt. "And I've got a feeling I know who!"

"Who?" said Bro.

"Look," said Squirt, pointing in a window, where three koala shapes were reflected – one wearing a monster mask, one wearing an alien mask and the other (the one doing the pointing) a pirate mask.

"Whoa," said Dude. "Who are those dudes?"

"Those dudes are us, Dude!" said Squirt.

"Uh?" said Dude. "They're not us!"

Squirt pulled off the pirate mask. "Ta-da!"

"Aw, yeah," said Bro, pulling off the alien mask. "Forgot about that."

"Totally forgot too, Bro," said Dude, pulling off the monster mask.

"Come back!" yelled an angry-sounding voice.

"Run for it!" yelled Squirt, chucking his mask behind him and setting off down the mall as fast as he could.

"No worries," said Bro, doing exactly the same.

"Totally," said Dude doing likewise.

Amazingly, no one seemed to notice the three koalas running headlong through the mall, weaving in and out of the legs of shoppers. Or at least, if they did, everyone was far too busy shopping to care.

"Come on!" yelled Squirt, turning round and seeing a line of kids heading their way.

"We're going as fast as we can, Squirt!" yelled Bro.

"Totally, mini-dude," yelled Dude. "We're right behind you!"

"Aw, Dude," panted Bro as they finally emerged from the mall into the warm sunshine. "Feel those rays."

"Mmmm, maybe we could just—" panted Dude.

"Not now," interrupted Squirt. "Look!"

Dude and Bro looked. A coach was parked outside the mall. The door was open. The driver was asleep.

"What are we waiting for?" said Squirt. "Let's go!"

Mustering up the last bit of energy they'd got, the three koalas ran to the

coach and scrambled up the steps before anyone spotted them. A few seconds later the air was filled with the sound of laughter and excited chatter as the kids boarded the coach and took their seats. Underneath one of the seats, Squirt, Dude and Bro snuggled together. It looked like the last leg of their journey was about to begin.

Chapter Eight

The coach rumbled on through the city, past tall, shining tower blocks, along streets full of shoppers and eventually over a muddy brown river flowing sluggishly towards the sea. But Squirt, Dude and Bro didn't see any of it. Huddled together in the gloom under the seat, they were unable to enjoy the view. The only view they had was of legs and trainers.

It was dark and dusty. Dark and dusty and pretty smelly too. Bread crumbs had been trodden into the carpet, along with bits of cheese and lettuce and tomato and cucumber and all kinds of flavours of crisps. Salt and vinegar, roast chicken, smoky bacon – but sadly, as far as the koalas were concerned anyway, no eucalyptus flavour.

Suddenly the coach slowed down to avoid something. The driver tooted his horn angrily before speeding back up again.

"Where are we?" said Bro, as if he'd just woken up.

"Dunno about you, Bro," said Dude, who actually *had* just woken up, "but I was in the middle of a totally awesome dream."

"You were *asleep?*" squeaked Squirt in amazement. "How could you sleep *now?*"

"Yeah, Dude," said Bro, stifling a yawn. "How could you sleep *now?*"

"Gimme a break, Bro," said Dude. "I just nodded off for a moment, that's all."

"We must be nearly there by now," said Squirt.

"How d'ya know that, Squirt?" said Bro.

"I don't know for sure," said Squirt. "But we've been driving for ages."

"We have?" said Dude.

"Yes!" said Squirt, firmly. "We have!"

"Right," said Dude. "Maybe I dropped off for a bit longer than a moment."

"Heh-heh-heh," chuckled Bro.

"Come to think of it, maybe it was more like a couple of moments," said Dude.

"I know one thing for sure, Dude," said Bro.

"What's that, Bro?" said Dude.

"I could fair chow down a nice juicy eucy branch."

"Aw, me too, Bro," said Dude.

"Well, we'll just have to wait, I'm afraid," said Squirt.

"How long?" said Bro.

"As long as it takes," said Squirt.

"As long as what takes?" said Dude.

Squirt was beginning to get more and more frustrated. "As long as it takes to get there!"

"Get where?" said Bro.

"The big zoo!" said Squirt.

"Aw, yeah," said Dude. "I remember now."

They remained huddled together in silence for a few moments until they heard a sound. It was rather a strange, muffled kind of sound. Strange, muffled and just a little bit sad. And it was coming from somewhere directly above.

"What's that?" said Bro.

"Haven't got a clue, Bro," said Dude.

"Only one way to find out," said Squirt,

scrambling out from under the seat.

There was a child sitting on the seat above. One child sitting on a seat built for two. It was a girl. And from what Squirt could see, she wasn't a very happy girl either. A solitary tear rolled down her cheek and she was sobbing softly to herself.

So that's *what the strange sound was*, thought Squirt. He wished she'd stop. He had no idea what was making the girl so sad, but whatever it was, was beginning to make him sad too. And now definitely wasn't the time to start feeling sad. Now was the time to maybe – just maybe – start feeling ever so slightly happier. They were on the way to the big zoo at last! It was what they'd been trying to do all day. Well – it was what Squirt had been trying to do all day anyway. Dude and Bro had largely spent the day either sleeping or moaning about how hungry they were!

The more Squirt looked at the girl, the more he knew he had to do something. Not only to make her happier, but to stop himself from becoming miserable. Koalas were good at cheering up humans. Squirt knew that. He knew that humans somehow found them cute and irresistible. He wasn't sure why this was the case. Why were koalas any more cute or irresistible than, say, crocodiles, or Tasmanian devils? But humans were strange creatures. Who knew what went on inside their heads?

"Psssssst!" said Bro, peering out from underneath the seat. "Get back under here, ya wallaby!"

"But she's really sad," said Squirt. "I've got to do something to help!"

"Are you crazy?" said Bro. "If they see us, they'll…"

But it was too late. Squirt was already tugging on the girl's dress. The girl looked down and gasped. Judging from her expression she could scarcely believe her eyes. She reached down and gently picked Squirt up. Instinctively, Squirt put his arms around her neck and gave her a big hug.

The girl immediately smiled and squeezed her eyes shut so tightly that two more tears rolled down her cheeks. But this time they weren't tears of sadness. This time they were tears of sheer happiness.

"Are you going to the zoo?" whispered the girl.

Squirt blinked his big koala eyes.

"Me too!" whispered the girl. "Will you be my friend? No one else will. They all think I'm weird and call me names just because I'm different and don't like all the things that they like. But I'm not weird. You don't think I'm weird, do you?"

Squirt blinked again.

"Will you be my friend?" whispered the girl. "Will you?"

Squirt blinked.

"Thank you," whispered the girl, snuggling into Squirt's neck.

Still peering out from underneath the

seat, Bro sniffed a couple of times.

"You OK, Bro?" said Dude.

"I'm fine, mate, no worries," said Bro, sniffing again.

"You're not crying, are you?" said Dude.

"Crying, Dude?" said Bro. "No, Dude. Just a speck of dust, Dude."

Dude looked at Bro for a moment.

"What?" said Bro. "I'm *not* crying!"

"Hey, no worries, Bro," said Dude. "No worries."

"It's the *dust*, Dude!" said Bro.

Dude sniffed. "You're right, Bro. It *is* a bit dusty down here."

But Dude had sniffed a bit too hard and immediately felt like he was about to sneeze.

"Ah-ah-ah-ah…" said Dude.

"Er, Dude, I wouldn't do that if I were you, mate," said Bro nervously.

"Ah-ah-ah-ah…" said Dude again.

"Seriously, Dude," said Bro. "We don't want the whole coach to…"

" A h - a h - a h - a h … AchoooOOOOOOO!!!" sneezed Dude.

The girl looked down to see Dude and Bro looking back up at her. She gave Squirt a quick glance. It was almost as if she knew what the little koala was thinking.

"Don't worry," she whispered. "I won't say anything."

A boy in the seat in front turned round, glaring at the girl. "Was that you?"

"Was that me, what?" said the girl.

"Sneezing," said the boy.

"Yes," said the girl, defiantly. "You got a problem with that?"

"Yes, I have got a problem with that, actually!" said the boy. "Keep your germs to yourself, ya weirdo!"

It was only then that the boy noticed Squirt, still with his arms round the girl's neck.

"Aw, how sweet!" sneered the boy sarcastically. "She's brought a cuddly toy with her!"

"So what?" said the girl, giving Squirt a stroke. "Nothing wrong with that."

The boy leaned closer to Squirt and

reached out to tickle him. "Coochy-coochy-coo!"

Squirt stuck his tongue out. The boy's face dropped like a stone.

"Aaaaaaaaaaagh!!!" screamed the boy.

The screaming boy pointed.

"Aaaaaaaaaagh!!!" screamed his friend when he turned round to see what the fuss was about.

"Aaaaaaaaaagh!!!" screamed two girls across the aisle when they looked over to see what the two boys were screaming at.

"Aaaaaaaaaagh!!!" screamed two more girls in front of them.

"Aaaaaaaaaagh!!!" screamed two more boys in front of *them*.

Before long the whole coach was in complete uproar. The screaming had spread like wildfire. The children had been excited enough in the first place, but now they were almost hysterical.

"OK, everybody! Quiet now! Calm down!" shouted a teacher from the front of the coach. "We'll be there in a minute!"

Sure enough the coach was slowing

down. Squirt looked at the girl.

"Thanks again," she grinned. "This is the best fun I've had for ages!"

Squirt blinked a couple of times and gave the girl an extra tight hug before disentangling himself from around her neck and hopping down to join Dude and Bro.

"Let's go!" he yelled above the din.

"No worries, Squirt!" yelled Bro, setting off towards the front of the coach.

"Totally, mini-dude!" yelled Dude, following.

Squirt lingered for a second, taking one last look up at his friend, before scurrying after the other two – whizzing under seats and zooming in and out of legs. Only the girl watched the koalas go. The other children were still too busy screaming to even notice.

They reached the front of the coach just as it stopped and the door hissed open. Dude, Bro and finally Squirt tumbled down the steps and out into the open air.

"Thought we'd lost you for a moment there, Squirt," said Bro.

"No chance," grinned Squirt.

"Heh-heh-heh," chuckled Dude.

"Heh-heh-heh," chuckled Bro.

"Whoa!" said Squirt.

"What?" said Bro.

"Look!" said Squirt.

"Where?" said Bro.

"*There!*" said Squirt.

Dude and Bro turned to find Squirt looking at a big wall. From beyond the wall there arose a cacophony of animal sounds. From above the wall there rose the tops of lots and lots of tall green trees. Dude and Bro sniffed the air.

"Is that what I think it is, Dude?" said Bro.

"What do you think it is, Bro?" said Dude.

"Eucalyptus, Dude," said Bro.

"Reckon you're right, Bro," said Dude.

Squirt turned to Dude and Bro in disbelief. "Is that all you can think about? Food?"

Dude and Bro looked at each other and shrugged.

"We've finally made it!" squeaked Squirt excitedly. "We've made it to the big zoo!"

Chapter Nine

"So, what now?" said Bro.

Squirt had to admit it. For once, Bro had actually asked a perfectly sensible question. What now? The obvious solution of course was to simply walk in through the main entrance to the zoo, along with all the visitors, and hope that no one noticed. But that was pretty unlikely, thought Squirt, and also pretty risky. If they got caught now, what would happen to them? Would they get taken to join Ma and Pa, or somewhere else entirely? If that happened they might have to start all over again! Ma and Pa would be worried for even longer! No, thought Squirt. The best bet was to finish the mission undercover. And besides, the whole day had been one big adventure! Why stop now?

"Come on, guys!" said Squirt, scurrying towards the wall as fast as he could.

"Where to?" said Dude, following.

"Over the wall before anyone sees us!" said Squirt.

"Then what?" said Bro, doing his best to keep up.

"I'm not sure," said Squirt.

"You're not sure?" said Bro.

"That's right, I'm not sure," said Squirt. "How about you have an idea for a change? Anybody would think *I* was the big brother here and *you* were the little brother!"

"Heh-heh-heh," chuckled Dude. "That's pretty funny, Bro."

"Glad you think so, Dude," said Bro, clearly annoyed.

They stopped when they reached the wall and looked up. It was very high. Not only that, but it was also very smooth.

Koalas were great climbers – but they weren't *that* great. Give them a tree to climb andthey'd be up there like a shot. But a wall like this, with no foot holds – or paw-holds – to cling to was another matter altogether.

"Can I help you?" said a deep voice.

"Aaaaaarrggghhh!!!" screamed Dude and Bro together.

"Who said that?" said Squirt, looking around anxiously.

"I did," said the deep voice.

"Where are you?" said Squirt.

"Up here."

The three koalas looked up to see a giraffe peering over the wall at them.

"Looks like you might need a lift," said the giraffe.

"A lift?" said Bro. "Where to?"

"Yeah, where to, mate?" said Dude. "We've only just got here!"

"Up in the air," said the giraffe.

"Up in the air?" said Bro.

"Over the wall," said the giraffe.

"Cool!" said Bro.

"Yes, please!" said Squirt. "That would be fantastic!"

"Totally," said Dude.

"No problem," said the giraffe, lowering his long neck down like a crane. "All aboard!"

One by one, Squirt, Bro and Dude put

their

front

paws round

the giraffe's neck,

just below his head.

"Hold tight," said the

giraffe, slowly raising his

neck back into the air again.

"Going up!"

And up they went. Higher

and higher. And the higher they went, the more difficult it became to hang on tightly. One by one the koalas slid down the giraffe's neck as if it was some kind of playground ride.

"Wheeeee!" squealed Dude.

"Wheeeee!" squealed Bro.

"Wheeeee!" squealed Squirt.

"That was fun, mate!" said Bro.

"Awesome!" said Dude. "Can we do it again?"

"Allow me," said the giraffe, lowering his neck again so that first Squirt, then Bro and finally Dude all slid the other way again before tumbling on to the ground in a heap.

"Heh-heh-heh," chuckled Bro.

"Heh-heh-heh," chuckled Dude.

"Thank you very much!" said Squirt.

"My pleasure," said the giraffe. "Is there anything else I can do for you?"

"Actually, there is," said Squirt.

"Fire away," said the giraffe.

"Can you tell us where the other koalas are, please?" said Squirt.

"Ah, I was afraid you were going to ask me that," said the giraffe.

Squirt was puzzled. "You were afraid I was going to ask you where the other koalas are?"

"No," said the giraffe. "I was afraid you might ask me where *anything* is!"

"Heh-heh-heh," chuckled Dude and Bro.

"Why?" said Squirt, giving them a dirty look.

"I don't *know* where anything is," said the giraffe, sadly.

"What? Nothing at all?" said Squirt.

The giraffe shook his head slowly. "I can't see anything because of all these tall trees."

Squirt looked up. The giraffe was right. The trees were very, very tall. Rather like the giraffe itself.

"I can munch a few branches? See if that helps?" said the giraffe. "It might take a while though."

"Thanks," said Squirt, "but we haven't

got that long. We're in a bit of a hurry! Gotta go!"

"See you later," said the giraffe. "Or maybe not."

"Byeeee!" called Squirt, scurrying off.

"Adios!" called Bro, scurrying after Squirt.

"Totally!" called Dude, scurrying after Bro.

***

"I wonder who lives here?" said Squirt, stopping next to an enclosure with a wall running around it.

"I do," said a squeaky voice from the other side of the wall.

Squirt couldn't see who the voice

belonged to, so he scrambled up the wall to get a better look. There he came face to face with a meerkat, standing on its back legs, trying to make itself as tall as possible.

"G'day," said Squirt.

"Hello," said the meerkat. "What's happening?"

"What do you mean, what's happening?" said Squirt. "What's happening where?"

"Anywhere," said the meerkat.

"*Anywhere?*" said Squirt.

"On the other side of the wall!" said the

meerkat. "I keep trying to look over it – but I'm not quite tall enough!"

Squirt sighed. What with giraffes who didn't know where anything was and meerkats who'd never seen anything, he was beginning to think they were never going to find the other koalas.

"I'm sorry," said Squirt.

"I *wish* I was taller," said the meerkat sadly.

Squirt wasn't sure what to say. He wasn't very tall himself, but he'd seen so much. He'd seen cars and lorries and coaches. He'd seen enormous shopping malls and tall buildings soaring into the sky like rockets. He'd seen green hills in the distance. He'd even seen the ocean. And that was just today!

"Tell me something you can see," said the meerkat. "Just one thing."

"Just one thing?" said Squirt.

The meerkat nodded.

"Anything at all?" said Squirt.

The meerkat nodded again.

Squirt looked around. "I can see my big brother and his friend."

"Really?" said the meerkat. "Where are they?"

"Under a tree," said Squirt.

"Under a tree?" said the meerkat. "What are they doing there?"

"Something that they shouldn't be doing," said Squirt.

"What's that?" said the meerkat.

"Trying to sleep!" said Squirt. "Gotta go! Catch you later!"

Squirt scrambled back down the wall, leaving the meerkat still desperately trying to peer over it.

"C'mon, you guys!" said Squirt. "You can't go to sleep now!"

"We can't?" said Bro, stifling a yawn.

"Not until we find Ma and Pa," said Squirt. "You can sleep all you want then!"

"Aw, mate, I can't wait," said Dude.

Squirt looked at Dude.

"I mean, I can't wait till we find yer ma and pa, obviously," said Dude. "Not till I go to sleep."

"Heh-heh-heh," chuckled Bro.

But Squirt wasn't listening any more. He'd spotted someone in the neighbouring enclosure who might just be able to help them. This particular enclosure wasn't full of tall trees. And this particular someone didn't actually *need* to be tall.

"Of course!" said Squirt. "Why didn't I think of that before?"

"Why didn't you think of what before?" said Bro.

"A kangaroo!" said Squirt. "It's perfect!"

"It is?" said Bro.

"What for?" said Dude.

"Look!" said Squirt.

Dude and Bro looked. Sure enough, a

kangaroo was bouncing up and down like kangaroos do. After watching the kangaroo bounce up and down for a minute, Dude and Bro started bouncing up and down too. They just couldn't help it.

"Heh-heh-heh," chuckled Bro.

"Heh-heh-heh," chuckled Dude.

"I hope you guys aren't making fun of me!" said the kangaroo, sternly.

"What?" said Bro, still bouncing. "No way, mate!"

"Aw, yeah, no way, mate!" said Dude, still bouncing. "We're just having a good time!"

"No offence, mate," said Bro.

The kangaroo suddenly burst out

laughing. "Just joking! Want to make a competition of it?"

"What do you mean?" said Bro.

"See who can bounce the highest?" said the kangaroo.

"Great idea!" said Squirt.

Bro didn't look convinced. "You reckon?"

"Of course!" said Squirt. "The higher you bounce the further you can see!"

"So?" said Bro, still not convinced.

"We're trying to find Ma and Pa, aren't we?"

"Yeah," said Bro.

"Well?" said Squirt. "Bounce high enough and you might even see them!"

"Aw, yeah!" said Dude. "The little feller's

right, mate! Come on!"

"S'pose so," said Bro.

And with that, Dude and Bro started bouncing even higher. But koalas are made for climbing trees – not for bouncing. No matter how hard Dude and Bro tried, they still couldn't bounce anywhere near as high as the kangaroo.

"Well?" said Squirt. "Can you see anything yet?"

"Not yet!" said Bro.

"Higher!" said Squirt. "Higher!"

Dude and Bro bounced even higher. But it was no good. They still couldn't bounce anywhere near as high as the kangaroo.

"Well?" said Squirt.

"Nothing yet, Squirt!" said Bro.

"I can see something!" said the kangaroo.

"Really?" said Squirt excitedly. "What?"

"I can see a keeper," said the kangaroo.

"A keeper?" said Squirt. "What's he doing?"

"Heading this way," said the kangaroo.

Squirt thought for a moment. A zoo keeper? Heading this way? That wasn't good. That wasn't good at all.

"That's enough bouncing, guys!"

"What?" yelled Bro.

"Stop bouncing!" yelled Squirt.

"Aw, do we have to?" yelled Dude. "This is totally awesome!"

"Yes!" yelled Squirt. "You have to! We've

174

got to get moving! Now!"

Dude and Bro reluctantly stopped bouncing.

"You win, mate," said Bro to the kangaroo.

"Heh-heh-heh," chuckled Dude.

"Watch out!" yelled the kangaroo.

But it was too late.

"Gotcha!" said a voice.

The next moment, Squirt, Dude and Bro found themselves caught up in a net and thrown into the back of a van. The door was slammed shut. Not for the first time that day, everything suddenly went very dark indeed.

Chapter Ten

Not *again*, thought Squirt. Not after everything they'd been through! It just wasn't fair. Where were they being taken to this time? What was going to happen to them when they got there? They'd been so close! Surely things weren't going to go wrong now, were they? A hundred different thoughts ran through Squirt's head. All of them bad.

"So…" began Bro.

"If you're going to ask me what we should do now, I'm going to scream!" said Squirt, cutting him off.

"I'm not sure that's a good idea, mini-dude," said Dude.

"What?" said Squirt.

"Not a good idea to start screaming, mini-dude."

Squirt sighed. "I didn't mean that's what I think we should do now! I meant that's what I'll do if he asks what we should do now, again!"

"Heh-heh-heh," chuckled Bro.

"It's *not* funny!" said Squirt. "Why should I have to make all the decisions? I'm fed up of making all the decisions!"

"Aw, you've been amazing, mini-dude," said Dude. "Isn't that right, Bro?"

There was no reply from Bro.

"I said, isn't that right, Bro? The little feller's been amazing?"

"S'pose so," muttered Bro.

"What do you mean, you *s'pose* so?" said Dude. "If it hadn't been for your little bro here, we'd have been back home hours ago!"

"Yeah, well, it looks like we're going back home now anyway, doesn't it?" said Bro.

"What d'ya mean, Bro?" said Dude. "You're not serious, are ya?"

"Where do *you* think we're going then?" said Bro.

Dude thought for a moment. He had no idea where they were going. All he could think about was sleeping and eating. And not necessarily in that order.

Squirt was beginning to wish that they *had* simply walked into the zoo through the main entrance with all the visitors after all, instead of trying to break in undetected. It might have been more exciting that way, but it looked like they could be in far worse trouble now.

The van suddenly slowed to a halt.

Squirt, Dude and Bro all held their breath in the dark. What was going to happen to them? They heard footsteps and then the sound of the door being opened.

"Come on, you three. Let's be having you," said the zoo keeper. Unsure what lay in store for them, the three koalas emerged, blinking in the bright sunlight, before hopping down on to the ground. It took several seconds for their eyesight to return to normal. They looked around. Where were they?

"Come on," laughed the zoo keeper. "Back you go now. And no more going walkabout!"

Squirt, Dude and Bro looked at each

other. Go where?

"Well," said the keeper. "Are you going, or not? I haven't got all day, ya know!"

The three koalas scampered through the gate into the enclosure and straight up the nearest tree.

"Ah, there you are, boys," said Mrs M as they appeared in the treetop.

Squirt, Dude and Bro slowly turned to each other in astonishment. They'd made it! They'd actually made it!

"What's up, boys?" laughed Mrs M. "You look like you've just seen a crocodile!"

Squirt was very confused. Why wasn't his mum more surprised? Or cross? Or both?

"Funny you should say that, Mrs M..." said Dude.

"Is it?" said Mrs M.

"Not really!" said Squirt quickly, before Dude could say anything else. It was beginning to look like they hadn't even been missed!

"But..." began Dude.

"Put a sock in it, ya wallaby!" hissed Bro.

"Heh-heh-heh," chuckled Squirt nervously. "You guys are hilarious!"

Mrs M looked at Squirt and smiled. "I think Squirty-Wirty needs a cuddly-wuddly!"

"Maaaaaaa!" said Squirt through gritted teeth.

"Aw, but you're so cute!" said Mrs M. "Isn't he, Mr M?"

But there was no response from Mr M. Exhausted from the move, Mr M was wedged between two branches, fast asleep. To be fair, Mr M would have been wedged between two branches, fast asleep, even if they *hadn't* moved. Mr M was sleepy even by koala standards. And that was saying something!

"Come on, now," said Mrs M. "Come to

Mumsy-Wumsy for a cuddly-wuddly!"

Squirt grinned. He didn't care if it *was* a bit embarrassing. A cuddle was *exactly* what he needed!

"Fancy a nice juicy eucy branch, boys?" said Mrs M.

"Never mind a branch, Ma," said Bro. "I could eat a whole tree!"

"Heh-heh-heh," chuckled Dude. "Me too, Mrs M."

"Help yourselves then," said Mrs M, still cuddling Squirt tightly. "I'd serve you myself but I'm a bit tied up here."

Dude and Bro didn't need telling twice, and helped themselves to a branch each.

"So?" said Mrs M. "What have you boys

been up to? I've not seen you since we got here!"

Squirt looked up at his ma. It was amazing. They really *hadn't* been missed at all!

"Well?" said Mrs M. "Is someone going to tell me, or not?"

"We missed the truck," said Dude between mouthfuls of eucalyptus.

"Pardon?" said Mrs M.

"We missed the truck, Mrs M," said Dude. "We were catching a few rays. By the time we woke up you'd already gone. So we borrowed a buggy from one of the keepers."

Mrs M smiled. "A buggy, eh?"

"Totally," said Dude. "We drove it up a ramp."

"A ramp?" said Mrs M. "Wow!"

Dude nodded. "Yeah. Straight into the back of a great big lorry."

"Oh, a lorry, eh?" laughed Mrs M, clearly not believing a single word Dude was saying. "Then what?"

"Well, we raced this old feller to a toy shop and then caught a bus here," said Dude. "Then a giraffe gave us a lift over the wall and we had a bouncing competition with a roo," said Dude.

"Course you did," chuckled Mrs M.

"We *did*!" insisted Dude.

"Such wonderful imagination," said Mrs M.

"I'm not imagining it, Mrs M!" said

Dude indignantly. "You can ask the little feller if you want!"

"Funny you should say that," said Mrs M.

"Is it, Ma?" said Squirt.

"You're not the littlest feller any more."

"I'm not?" said Squirt.

"He's not?" said Bro.

"Meet your baby sister, boys," beamed Mrs M.

Squirt gasped as a tiny head poked out of his ma's pouch.

With all the excitement, he'd quite forgotten that she was having a baby! Squirt's heart melted in an instant. Everything else suddenly seemed very unimportant.

"Isn't she a beaut?" said Mr M, finally waking up.

"Aw, yeah," said Bro.

"Totally!" said Dude.

"Aren't you going to say something?" said Mrs M to Squirt.

But Squirt was utterly speechless. Not only was his baby sister impossibly cute and gorgeous – more importantly, he was now no longer the youngest in the family! No matter how annoying she grew up to be in years to come, Squirt would always be grateful to his little sister for that!

"Well?" said Mrs M.

"She's… she's… she's…" said Squirt.

"What?" yawned Bro.

"What?" yawned Dude.

"Just perfect," yawned Squirt, the day finally beginning to catch up with him, his eyelids gradually getting heavier and heavier.

"Looks like you boys need to get some kip," said Mr M.

"I'm not surprised!" laughed Mrs M. "All those adventures they've been having!"

Mr M winked.

"Heh-heh-heh," chuckled Bro.

"Heh-heh-heh," chuckled Dude.

"What's so funny?" said Mrs M.

"Nothing, Ma," said Squirt quickly.

"Come on then, Mr M," said Mrs M, heading off with the new baby. "Let's leave them to it."

"Right behind you, Mrs M," said Mr M, following.

***

"Well, we made it, Dude!" said Bro, once they were alone.

"We totally did, Bro!" said Dude. "We totally did!"

"Well done, Squirt," said Bro. "We really couldn't have done it without you."

Squirt couldn't quite believe his ears. "Are you talking to me?"

"Well, I'm not talking to *him*," yawned Bro, looking at Dude. "He's been about as much use a straight boomerang!"

Squirt waited, expecting to hear Dude chuckle. But he didn't. Dude had fallen fast asleep.

"A straight boomerang," laughed Squirt. "That's funny."

But Bro didn't say anything. He'd fallen fast asleep too.

Squirt stretched and yawned. It was high time he joined them.